THE FIRE TRUCK WHO GOT LOST

Words and Story by

COLIN ELDRED-COHEN

Illustrations by

AMBER DE JOYA

To Atticus and Sebastian,

my favorite little firefighters

AUTISM CREATIVES COLLECTIVE

The Autism Creatives Collective (ACC) is a community of talented creative writers, artists and musicians on the Autism spectrum. The ACC identifies opportunities and supports these writers, artists, musicians and story tellers to find jobs, careers and other ways to share their creativity with the world. The ACC develops partnerships to help industries, employers and others take advantage of extraordinary talents of the ACC community. The ACC is a project of AASCEND.

ISBN-13: 978-1535429061

This Book Belongs To:

_____

FIREFIGHTER

MEET THE TRUCKS!

BARNABUS

Our young fire truck grew up in Fire Station 12 with all the bigger trucks helping to raise him together. He's not old enough to fight fires yet, but he still loves learning and being with his fire truck family.

AGUA

Agua transferred in from a city to the south and is in charge of the fire station water supply. She's very good with numbers and details, so she always knows when the water isn't where it should be.

HOGWASH

Hogwash likes to stick to procedure, mostly because he's the oldest engine. That doesn't mean the other trucks don't like him, he's just very strict. But it's that strictness that keeps Fire Station 12 running so successfully.

YOUR BEST FRIENDS ON WHEELS!

WHEELIE DAN

Wheelie Dan is an upstanding fellow who hurt his wheel while saving people from a fire. He can still roll with the best of them, but if you look closely, you can see the bandage that keeps his wheel from leaking. He really likes that wheel.

TURPENTINE

Turpentine is a fun-loving engine and likes to show off sometimes, but she still does her job very well. She loves to play games with Barnabus and play tricks on the other trucks sometimes. She started out in some small country towns where she picked up the grass she has in her mouth.

THE BIG DALMATIAN

This massive pooch has been around the station for as long as Barnabus can remember. Apart from being helpful and playful, the Big Dalmatian also gets really worried when the trucks don't come back when they're supposed to.

Once, there was a little fire truck named Barnabus. He lived with the other fire trucks down at the fire station with their Big Dalmatian.

There were four big engines, Hogwash, Wheelie Dan, Agua, and Turpentine.

It was their job to drive the firefighters to where there was a fire and help them put it out.

"Someday, I'm going to be just like them," Barnabus would say.

One night, there was a big fire downtown, so all of the trucks got ready to drive out.

"Barnabus," Aqua asked him, "would you like to come with us and watch?"

"Of course I would!" Barnabus said with a big grin. He was so excited!

They all rolled around the huge office building and started spraying it with their hoses. Barnabus tried to help out, but his hose was small and didn't have a lot of water.

"I know!" Barnabus said. "I'll find a fire hydrant to get more water!"

So he drove away to look for one.

While he was gone, the other engines finally put out the fire.

"Good work!" they said and started driving back to the station.

But nobody noticed that Barnabus was missing!

Barnabus came back to the building with more water, but no one was there!
"Hello?" he called out, wondering where everyone was.

"Where is everyone?" he wondered as he drove around looking for his friends.

He drove through downtown.
He drove around the hardware store.
He even drove past the ballpark.

But he couldn't find the other trucks.
Even worse, he didn't know how to find the
fire station. "I'm lost," he said sadly.

Back at the station, the other trucks noticed that someone was missing. "Where's Barnabus?" asked Wheelie Dan.

"We must have left him!" yelled Agua.

With no time to lose, the trucks drove out and began searching the city.

Meanwhile, Barnabus was still by himself.
He would ask someone where the station
was, but everyone was asleep.

"I have an idea," he said. "I'll call the other trucks with my siren!"

He turned on his siren, but it was little so it couldn't make a lot of noise.

Just as he was about to turn it off, he heard a dog barking at him from down the block. The siren must have woken him up.

"I have another idea!"

Barnabus drove around for a bit until he found a street with some big apartment buildings on both sides.

He turned on his siren again, as loud as he could. Soon, everyone living in the apartments were turning on their lights to see what was going on.

Far off, the engines saw all the lights from the apartments. "What's that?" asked Turpentine.

They drove over to find out.

There was Barnabus!

All the engines happily gathered around him. "I'm sorry," said Barnabus, "I just wanted to help out with the fire."

"We're sorry too!" said Turpentine.
"Next time, let's check in with each
other before we go anywhere."

So they all went back to the station and went
to sleep. Barnabus was in his little corner,
smiling in his sleep, curled up with
the Big Dalmatian.

Colin Eldred-Cohen is a creative writer and storyteller. He was born in San Diego and graduated from the San Diego School for Creative and Performing Arts (SCPA), where he discovered his talents for performing, singing and Irish dance. He graduated from UC Santa Cruz with a degree in film.

He is currently living in San Jose where he is writing regularly for FishandCherries.com and putting his writing talents to use working on his first novel (that he hopes will be a bestseller, made into an Oscar-winning movie and a line of happy meal toys.)

Colin is on the Autism spectrum, and has channeled his creative and active mind to become a talented writer and storyteller. He is an active member of the Autism Creatives Collective.

The Fire Truck Who Got Lost is his first children's book.

Amber de Joya is a talented illustrator and freelance artist originally from the Philippines.

She graduated from UC Santa Cruz with a Fine Art degree. Her illustrations are inspired by Disney, Pixar and many other artists.

She currently lives in the San Francisco Bay Area with her 10 year old puppy and jumps out of airplanes in her spare time.

Made in the USA
San Bernardino, CA
07 February 2017